iVy + bEAN
BOOK ❷

More Praise for Ivy + Bean!

★ "Just right for kids moving on from beginning readers . . . illustrations deftly capture the girls' personalities and the tale's humor. . . . Barrows' narrative brims with sprightly dialogue."
— *Publishers Weekly*, starred review

★ "In the tradition of Betsy and Tacy, Ginnie and Genevra, come two new friends, Ivy and Bean. . . . The deliciousness is in the details here. . . . Will make readers giggle."
— *Booklist*, starred review

"A charming new series." —*People*

"Ivy and Bean are a terrific buddy combo." —*Chicago Tribune*

"Readers will be snickering in glee over Ivy and Bean's antics."
—*Kirkus Reviews*

"This is a great chapter book for students who have recently crossed the independent reader bridge."
—*School Library Journal*

"Annie Barrows' simple and sassy text will draw in both thereluctant reader and the young bookworm. Fans of Beverly Cleary's Beezus and Ramona will enjoy this cleverly written and illustrated tale of sibling rivalry and unexpected friendship."
—*BookPage*

iVy + BEAN

AND THE GHOST THAT HAD TO GO

BOOK 2

written by annie barrows + illustrated by sophie blackall

chronicle books · san francisco

For Esme, finally —A. B.

For Ms. Wissot, who is the best kind of teacher —S. B.

First paperback edition published in 2007 by Chronicle Books LLC.

Text © 2006 by Annie Barrows.
Illustrations © 2006 by Sophie Blackall.

Book design by Sara Gillingham.
Typeset in Candida.
The illustrations in this book were rendered in Chinese ink.
Manufactured in China.
ISBN-13 978-0-8118-4911-1

The Library of Congress has catalogued the hardcover edition as follows:
Barrows, Annie.
Ivy and Bean and the ghost that had to go /
by Annie Barrows ; illustrated by Sophie Blackall.
p. cm.
Summary: Second-graders Ivy and Bean set out to expel the
ghost who is living in the girls' bathroom at their school.
ISBN-13: 978-0-8118-4910-4
ISBN-10: 0-8118-4910-4
[1. Best friends—Fiction. 2. Friendship—Fiction.
3. Ghosts—Fiction. 4. Bathrooms—Fiction. 5. Schools—Fiction.]
I. Title: Ghost that had to go. II. Blackall, Sophie, ill. III. Title.
PZ7.B27576Jg 2006
[Fic]—dc22
2005031790

25 24 23 22

Chronicle Books LLC
680 Second Street, San Francisco, California 94107

www.chroniclekids.com

CONTENTS

THE GYMNASTICS CLUB

One, two, three, four, five, six, seven, eight, nine, ten—*wham*! Bean crashed into the grass.

"Ouch," said Ivy, peeking through a hole in her sandwich. "Doesn't that hurt?"

"No. I'm just dizzy," said Bean. She sat up, and the playground began to tilt. Ugh. She lay down again.

Now Emma stood up. She lifted her hands above her head, took a big breath, and began. She did nine good cartwheels before she fell on her head.

"Are you all right?" Ivy asked Emma with her mouth full of peanut butter.

"Sort of," said Emma.

Now it was Zuzu's turn. Zuzu was the best cartwheeler in the Gymnastics Club. She was also the best backbender. She could do seven round-offs in a row. Nobody else could do even one.

Zuzu pulled down her ruffled pink shirt and raised her hands. One, two, three, four, five, six, seven, eight, nine, ten, *eleven*, *twelve* cartwheels, and still Zuzu landed on her feet. Then she arched over backward. She flung her arms over her head and made a perfect back-bend. She looked like a turned-over pink teacup. Then she rose back up—*boing*—like a doll with elastic in its legs.

"Wow," said Ivy.

Bean jumped up. She just *had* to do twelve cartwheels.

"Stand back!" she yelled.

"Wait," said Zuzu. "What about Ivy? Aren't you going to do a cart-wheel, Ivy?"

"I'm guarding the jackets," said Ivy.

"But Ivy, this is the Gymnastics Club," said Zuzu. "You can't just guard jackets."

Why not? Ivy wondered.

"We'll teach you how to do it if you don't know," said Emma.

"She knows," said Bean. "She can do a cartwheel. I've seen her."

Ivy looked at Bean in surprise. Why was she saying that? Ivy had never done a cartwheel in her life. Slowly, Ivy put her sandwich down next to Emma's jacket. "There's just one little problem—" she began.

"Hey, Leo!" yelled Bean suddenly. "You'd better watch out! If I get hit with that ball, there's going to be trouble!"

Leo was the leader of the soccer kids at

Emerson School. Before there was a Gymnastics Club, the soccer kids had the whole field to themselves during lunch recess. When Bean and Emma and Zuzu and Ivy started the Gymnastics Club, they kept getting hit with soccer balls. One day, Bean got clobbered in the stomach, and she declared war on the soccer kids. She came to school

with a bag of
ripe plums and chased
Leo down. When she caught him, she sat on
him and rubbed plums into his hair. Rose the
Yard Duty had been really mad. She told Leo
and Bean that they had to work it out, or she
would kick them all off the field.

So Bean and Leo worked it out. The Gymnastics Club was supposed to have all the grass near the play structure. The soccer kids were supposed to keep their balls from hitting the Gymnastics Club. Bean promised not to bring plums to school anymore. After that, the war was mostly over.

But now Leo looked mad. "It's not even near you!" he yelled. He was right. The ball was on the other side of the field, near MacAdam, a weird kid who sat under the trees and ate dirt when he thought no one was looking.

"Okay!" yelled Bean,

feeling like a dork. She had only been trying to help Ivy.

"Like I was saying, I can't do a cartwheel at the moment," said Ivy.

"Why?" asked Zuzu with her hands on her hips.

"Because," Ivy said, "we've got an emergency situation going on. Right over there." She pointed.

Emma, Zuzu, and Bean followed Ivy's pointing finger across the playground. She was pointing directly to the girls' bathroom. The one right outside their classroom.

THE OATH OF LIQUIDS

"What?" said Emma.

"What?" said Zuzu.

"You don't see it?" said Ivy.

"What are you talking about?" asked Emma.

Bean didn't say anything. She was watching Ivy. What was going on?

"I see a bathroom. I don't see any emergency situation," said Zuzu. She patted the little pink bow in her hair.

Ivy stopped pointing and sighed. "Oh well. You probably wouldn't believe me, anyway."

"I'd believe you," said Bean. "Anyway, you have to tell me because of the oath."

Two Saturdays before, Ivy had told Bean about blood oaths. If you write down a promise and sign it with your own blood, then you have to keep the promise always. If you didn't, the blood inside your body would curdle. Bean didn't know what curdling was, so Ivy explained that it was like cottage cheese. How disgusting was that? Bean was ready to give it a try right away, but first they had to think of an oath. Bean wanted the oath to be about turning her older sister Nancy to stone, maybe not forever, but for a month at least. Ivy said no. It had to be something they could do for sure.

In the end, they promised to tell each other all their secrets for the rest of their lives. Ivy wrote the words down with a silver marker. It looked very fancy. The problem was that the oath had to be signed at midnight. They tried for three days. Ivy tried staying awake until midnight. Bean tried waking herself up at midnight. They both tried sleeping on the floor, so that they would be really uncomfortable and wake up. Nothing worked.

Ivy said it would be almost the same if they did it at the stroke of noon. The two girls squished into Bean's old playhouse, and Ivy read the oath in a very serious voice. Then she got out a pin. She held it right above her finger, ready to stab herself. Almost ready to stab herself.

"Blood attracts vampire bats," she said suddenly.

"Vampire bats?" said Bean.

"Yeah. Vampire bats. They drink blood. Mostly, they drink cow blood, but they might get attracted to us if we sign the oath with blood." She put the pin down.

Bean understood. Poking your finger with a pin didn't seem like a big deal until you were about to do it. She didn't really want to poke her own finger, either.

But they both felt disappointed. A blood oath had been such a great idea.

"Why does it have to be blood?" asked Bean. "Why couldn't it be something else from inside us?"

"Like what?" Ivy looked interested. "Boogers?"

"Yuck," said Bean. "No. What about spit?"

Ivy said, "Spit would be all right, I guess. I don't want my spit to curdle, either."

Bean and Ivy never got much chance to spit because their mothers didn't like it. So they each made a big one and gooshed it around into letters. They had more spit than they knew what to do with. The paper tore in one place. And you couldn't really see their names when it dried. "That just makes it more mysterious," Bean said.

"It's an oath of liquids," said Ivy. "A powerful oath."

So now Ivy had to tell her secret to Bean.

"Excuse me," said Ivy politely to Emma and Zuzu. She pulled Bean a few steps away. "This morning," whispered Ivy, "when I went to the bathroom, I got a funny feeling, like I was walking through a cold mist. And even though it was warm, I began to shiver. My teeth were chattering, like this." Ivy smacked her teeth together. "And then I heard this strange whining noise, like this." Ivy squealed with her mouth closed.

Bean didn't know what she was talking about. "Was it someone locked in a stall?" she guessed.

"No! Don't you get it?" Ivy's eyes glowed.

"Get what?"

"It's a ghost! The bathroom is haunted!" Ivy whisper-shouted.

Bean spun around to look at the school. The long, open breezeway was dotted with blue doors. The first- and second-grade girls' bathroom was in the middle of the breeze-way. Bean could see a girl coming out of the bathroom door right now.

"Look!" Ivy grabbed her arm. "See the cloudy stuff right next to that girl's head? See?" Bean squinted. The more she squinted, the more she could see a pale, milky cloud

floating on the side of the bathroom door.
The girl, stepping out into the breezeway,
rubbed her arms. "See!" Ivy squeaked. "See!
She's cold because she just walked through
a ghost."

And then Bean could see it clearly. The
pale spot grew thicker, until it was a patch of
fog about the size of a person. You couldn't
see through it to the inside of the bathroom.
"I can see it," whispered Bean. "Does it have
yellowish eyes? Like little flashlights?"

"Yes!" Ivy whispered, squeezing Bean's arm. "Yes, it does!"

They looked at each other and smiled. This was even better than a blood oath. "How totally cool!" shouted Bean. A haunted bathroom! In her own school!

"What's cool?" yelled Emma and Zuzu together. "Tell us!"

But at that minute, the bell rang. Lunch was over.

"We'll tell," said Ivy. "Right here. After school."

"You're going to love it!" said Bean.

WHO'S THAT UGLY GUY?

Even before Ivy and Bean were friends, they had both been in Ms. Aruba-Tate's second-grade class. They didn't sit together. But after the day they threw worms at Bean's sister Nancy, they asked Ms. Aruba-Tate if they could share a table. Ms. Aruba-Tate just loved it when people were friends. She smiled and said, "That's wonderful, girls! The two of you will be a great team!" After a minute, though, she added, "But if there's talking, I'm going to have to separate you."

So far, Ivy and Bean had been separated six times.

This was not a big surprise. Bean had been separated from everyone in the class at least once. No matter who she sat next to, Bean talked.

Even MacAdam, who mostly talked to him-
self, had to be separated from Bean. Once,
Ms. Aruba-Tate had Bean sit by herself, but
Bean just talked louder.

Bean *tried* not to talk. She promised not to
talk. But every day she talked. Mostly, she
was trying to be helpful. She was trying to
explain things to kids who didn't understand.
For example, regrouping. Eric didn't understand
regrouping. Ms. Aruba-Tate had explained it,
but he didn't understand it. So he added
instead of subtracting. Bean couldn't stand to
watch him add when she knew he was supposed to subtract. Just knowing that he was
adding made it impossible for her to do her
own subtraction. She had to tell him that he
was doing it wrong. She had to tell him how
to do it right.

"Bean is only responsible for Bean," Ms. Aruba-Tate kept saying. But Bean thought that wasn't true, because Ms. Aruba-Tate also kept saying that a class was like a family. And families were responsible for each other. When Bean pointed this out, Ms. Aruba-Tate opened her mouth and then closed it again.

Ivy was very quiet. She was the quietest kid in the class. So Ms. Aruba-Tate kept putting Bean back with Ivy. "I think she hopes it will rub off on me," Bean explained to her mom. "But so far, it hasn't."

Even though she hadn't learned how to be quiet, Bean

had learned a lot by sitting next to Ivy. One thing she had learned was that Ivy wasn't as quiet as she seemed. Ivy talked. She just talked so softly that no one could hear her.

After lunch, the second-graders had science. They were doing a unit on dinosaurs. Bean's favorites were the ones that had big, bony skulls they cracked together when they fought. Ivy liked the bird-dinosaurs with feathers and sharp claws and red eyeballs. Today, the second-graders were learning about swimming dinosaurs. Actually, they weren't dinosaurs at all. Ms. Aruba-Tate was saying, "These prehistoric creatures are called *marine reptiles*. One marine reptile is—"

"Pteranodon!" Eric hollered, waving his arm in the air.

"Plesiosaur," breathed Ivy so only Bean could hear her.

"Plesiosaur," said Bean out loud.

"I like the way that Emma is raising her hand. Emma?" said Ms. Aruba-Tate.

Emma stared at her. "Um. I forget."

Ms. Aruba-Tate said, "Bean, will you repeat what you said?"

"Plesiosaur," said Bean. "Ivy said it, really."

"Thank you, Ivy and Bean," said Ms. Aruba-Tate. Then she held up a picture of something that looked like a whale and a giraffe glued together.

"Who's that ugly guy?" Dusit shouted. Then he laughed so hard that he fell out of his chair.

"Dusit, will you please go sit on the rug?" said Ms. Aruba-Tate.

"Do sit, Dusit!" hollered Eric. He fell out of his chair, too.

Ms. Aruba-Tate put the picture down in her lap. "Class, if you can't make more mature decisions, I will have to put our marine reptile materials away," she said. "Is that what I should do?"

"Noooooooo," the second grade muttered, feeling ashamed. They loved marine reptiles and they loved Ms. Aruba-Tate.

Ms. Aruba-Tate smiled. She held up the picture. "Now, the largest of the Plesiosaurs was the Elasmosaur. As you can see in this picture, it had an extremely long neck.

Does anyone have a *theory* about why such a long neck would be useful?"

"You could wrap it around somebody's body and squeeze them until they were dead!" yelled Drew. "Like this!" He put his arm around Vanessa's neck and began to squeeze.

"Drew! Stop that!"

"I wasn't going to do it for real! I was just showing!"

Bean raised her hand. "Maybe they could reach up out of the water and eat birds or something."

"That's an interesting theory, Bean," said Ms. Aruba-Tate. "Does anyone else have a theory?"

"Other way around," Ivy murmured.

"What?" said Bean.

"They reached down under the water," breathed Ivy.

"Ivy has a theory, Ms. Aruba-Tate," said Bean.

"Do you want to share it with the rest of us, Ivy?" asked Ms. Aruba-Tate.

"The Elasmosaur probably used its long neck to go down to the seafloor and eat stuff there," said Ivy softly.

"Very good thinking, you two!" Ms. Aruba-Tate smiled. "And Drew, your theory may be correct as well—please leave Vanessa alone—but unfortunately we have no way of proving these theories one way or the other since the Elasmosaur is—what's the word, boys and girls?"

"Extinct!" they hollered.

"Except for the Loch Ness monster," said Ivy softly.

"Yes, Ivy?" said Ms. Aruba-Tate. "Can you name another type of marine reptile?"

"Uh," said Ivy. She was stuck. Ms. Aruba-Tate probably didn't believe in the Loch Ness monster. Ivy couldn't think of any other marine reptiles. "I said, Can I go to the bathroom?"

"Oh!" said Ms. Aruba-Tate. "Go along."

After the door had closed behind Ivy, Bean waved her hand in the air. "Ms. Aruba-Tate, I have to go, too."

"Are you sure, Bean?" asked Ms. Aruba-Tate.

"Yes! Bad!" Bean held her breath, trying to turn her face red. If your face was red, Ms. Aruba-Tate usually let you go.

Ms. Aruba-Tate still looked doubtful. "Go on then. But come back ASAP." ASAP was Ms. Aruba-Tate's word for *fast*.

THE PORTAL

Ivy was standing outside the bathroom door. She was staring at the ground.

"Whatcha looking at?" asked Bean.

"Portal," said Ivy, pointing to a whitish stain on the cement.

"What?"

"It's a portal. A door. To the underworld. This is where the ghost is coming in." Ivy kneeled down to touch the stain.

Bean felt a little shiver on the back of her head. A haunted bathroom was cool, but a door to the underworld was creepy. The stain *did* kind of look like a ghost. She didn't feel so excited about the ghost anymore. "Why would a ghost come to our bathroom, anyway?" she asked, kneeling beside Ivy.

"The school was probably built on top of graves," said Ivy. "When they do that, it disturbs the spirits, so they wander around, all sad and miserable, haunting whatever was built on top of them."

"But it's not our fault. We didn't decide to build the school here."

Ivy shook her head. "Ghosts don't care." Her

voice got mysterious. "And now they will seek revenge on the intruders who ruined their graves."

"Revenge," said Bean, staring at the spot. She imagined cloudy shapes whirling down the breezeway toward Ms. Aruba-Tate's classroom.

"They'll be pouring in," said Ivy. "An army of ghosts."

"But there's just one now, right?" asked Bean quickly.

Ivy jumped up. "Let's find out," she said, reaching for the door.

An army of ghosts! No way Bean was going in that bathroom now. "Ms. Aruba-Tate said we had to come back ASAP," she said.

Ivy saw Bean's face. "Oh, okay," she said. "Let's go back."

+ + + + + +

"Put up your chairs, boys and girls," said Ms. Aruba-Tate. She said it every afternoon  when the bell rang, and every afternoon, half the class forgot. "Drew, please keep your hands to yourself. MacAdam, you may not put the turtle in your backpack. Thank you."

Emma and Zuzu were already on the field when Ivy and Bean got there. They weren't doing cartwheels. They were just waiting.

"So?" said Emma. "Tell us."

Ivy explained about the milky cloud,

about the girl coming out of the bathroom shivering, about the moaning noise, and about the yellow eyes that shone like flashlights. When she was done, Emma and Zuzu turned to look at the blue bathroom door.

"No way," said Zuzu.

"I don't see anything," said Emma.

"That's okay. Some people just can't see them," said Ivy. "Bean can."

Bean nodded. Some people couldn't see them, but she could.

"But wait," said Emma. "If there's a ghost, I want to see it." She leaned forward, staring at the bathroom.

"Keep your eyes open for a long time without blinking," Ivy suggested.

Emma popped her eyes at the door.

A girl ran down the breezeway and into the bathroom. As the door swung shut, Emma said, "I see a cloud! It's a milky cloud, like you said!"

"Yeah. That's it," Ivy said, nodding.

Zuzu popped her eyes, too. "Is it glowing? I thought I saw something glowing."

"That's the eyes," Bean said. "You must be seeing its eyes." She felt important, helping Zuzu to see the ghost.

"What are you guys doing?" It was Leo, with a soccer ball under his arm.

"Look!" said Ivy, pointing. The girl was coming out of the bathroom. "See how she's rubbing her hands? That's because she just walked through the cold mist. She's probably shivering, too!"

Leo looked at Ivy. "What?"

"There's a ghost in our bathroom," Bean explained.

"It's like walking through a cold mist," said Emma.

"And it has glowing eyes," added Zuzu.

"You guys are wacko," said Leo, dropping his ball on the ground and pretending to kick it.

"There's a portal to the ghost world right outside the door, in the cement," said Ivy to Emma and Zuzu. "Bean and I found it when we went to the bathroom. Come on. I'll show it to you."

"A portal?" said Emma. "What's a portal?"

"It's a doorway to the underworld," Bean explained.

"Oh." Emma stood still.

Bean understood how she felt. "We're not going in," she explained. "We're just looking at the portal."

"It will be totally safe," said Ivy.

Bean knew that Ivy thought almost anything was safe.

"Okay," said Emma. Zuzu nodded.

They started across the playground. Leo followed along, kicking the ball as he went.

ZUZU SPILLS THE BEANS

The next day at lunch recess, there were no gymnastics on the grass. No soccer, either. Every second-grader in the school gathered around the play structure, watching the bathroom. Whenever someone went in, they could see the ghost inside. It had definitely become clearer during the night.

Pretty soon, nobody went in. Everyone knew about the ghost, even the kindergartners, and nobody wanted to use a haunted bathroom. Still, the second-graders kept watching the door, just in case an army of ghosts floated out.

"What are you kids doing?" yelled Rose the Yard Duty.

"We're just standing here," Bean yelled back. "It's a free country."

"You watch it, Miss Bean," warned Rose, but she went away.

The ghost didn't start causing problems until that afternoon.

It was right in the middle of Drop Everything and Read when Ms. Aruba-Tate's classroom door burst open. Mrs. Noble marched in, holding Zuzu by the shoulder. Mrs. Noble was a fifth-grade teacher. She had a thousand tiny wrinkles on her face,

and she wore high heels and stockings every day. Bean's mother said that Mrs. Noble was an "old-fashioned teacher." Bean's sister Nancy said that Mrs. Noble locked kids in her art cupboard when they were bad. Bean's mother said that Nancy was exaggerating. That was a nice way to say lying.

Bean put her book down. She didn't like Drop Everything and Read anyway, except for the beginning, when she got to drop things. Mrs. Noble's high heels were red with stiff black bows at the front, and her shiny red fingernails were pressed into Zuzu's shoulder. Zuzu was about to cry. This was going to be much more interesting than a book.

Mrs. Noble didn't bother to lower her voice. "Becky," she boomed, "you've got to keep an eye on them! I found this one all the way over in the upper-school bathroom."

Ms. Aruba-Tate looked worried. "What were you doing in the upper-school bathroom, honey?"

Zuzu opened her mouth, but no sound came out. Big tears dripped down her cheeks and fell on the floor. "Our bathroom's h-h-haunted!" she wailed suddenly.

Oh brother. Bean looked sideways at Ivy. Trouble.

Ivy was staring at Zuzu.

Then Zuzu pointed right at Ivy and Bean. "They—they—they saw a ghost in the

bathroom, and it's
mad because the
school's on top of its grave,
and there's a portal, and more
ghosts are coming!" she gasped.

Ivy slid down in her chair until she could
hardly see over the desktop.

Ms. Aruba-Tate put her arms around Zuzu.
"Honey, the bathroom's not haunted—"

"Oh yes it is!" hollered Eric.

"I saw him!" yelled Dusit.

"He's got yellow, glowing eyes, Ms. Aruba-Tate," said Vanessa. "Ivy says."

Ivy looked at the classroom door. If she ran for it, would Ms. Aruba-Tate catch her before she got out?

Ms. Aruba-Tate turned to Ivy. "Is all this coming from you, Ivy?" She sounded like she couldn't believe it.

Ivy swallowed. She wished she had never seen the ghost. She wished she had never said the word *ghost.* "All what?" she said finally, in a high voice.

Ms. Aruba-Tate looked over the class. "Boys and girls, who has heard this silly story?"

One by one, the hands went up, until only Ivy's were in her lap.

"Ivy," said Ms. Aruba-Tate, "are you going to tell me that you have no idea what Zuzu is talking about?"

"No," said Ivy softly, her eyes on her desk. "It's not a silly story. The bathroom *is* haunted." Her face was burning hot.

Oh boy, thought Bean. Trouble with cheese on top.

Mrs. Noble shook her head. "Smart-aleck," she boomed. "I'd send her to the Principal if she were mine, Becky."

"Ooooooh," murmured the second grade.

But, as it turned out, Ms. Aruba-Tate didn't send Ivy to the Principal's Office. Instead, the whole class sat in a circle on the rug while Ms. Aruba-Tate talked about

how important imagination was. Then Ms. Aruba-Tate told them a story about yelling "Fire!" in a crowded theater. Bean had no idea what any of it had to do with a haunted bathroom. Ivy just wanted to run away. She didn't hear anything. At least, not until Ms. Aruba-Tate said, "Some stories can be harmful to others, class, and that means we have to use our imaginations responsibly and respectfully."

Ivy tried to scrunch down behind Bean, who was sitting next to her.

Ms. Aruba-Tate said, "Do you understand, Ivy?"

"Yes," whispered Ivy, not looking at Ms. Aruba-Tate.

The bell rang and everybody started squirming around, but Ms. Aruba-Tate held up her hand. "So I expect that I won't hear any more nonsense about a ghost in the bathroom. Right?"

Everyone looked at Ivy. Ivy picked some dirt out of the rug. "Right," she whispered after a moment.

"Put up your chairs, boys and girls," said Ms. Aruba-Tate.

NO MORE NONSENSE

Ivy wasn't exactly crying, but her eyes were glittery.

"She still likes you," Bean said. "Really, she does."

Ivy shook her head. They were supposed to be walking home, but Ivy kept stopping. She felt too awful to walk.

"Why didn't you just say that the bathroom wasn't haunted?" asked Bean. "Grown-ups never like that kind of stuff."

"But it *is* haunted," Ivy said. "And I'm the one who said it was."

"Okay," Bean said. "But you don't have to tell them everything."

"I didn't think Ms. Aruba-Tate would get mad at me."

"She's not mad at you," said Bean.

"She *is* mad at me," said Ivy in a choked voice. "She hates me."

"No. She likes you because you know all the answers," Bean said.

Ivy didn't say anything, but she started walking again.

"Ivy's in trouble!" sang a voice behind them.

Bean whirled around. "Why don't you just *shut up*, Leo?!"

"Hey!" said Leo, surprised. "That's mean."

"Go away," Bean said. She wished she had some plums.

"I live on this street, you doof." Leo picked up a rock and threw it at a tree. "I heard you got sent to the Principal's," he said to Ivy.

"I did *not!*" yelled Ivy. She stuck her tongue out at Leo.

"Jeez," said Leo. "If there is a ghost, your ugly face will scare him back to his grave."

Ivy stopped sticking out her tongue. "Oh!" she said. "Bean! That's what we have to do!"

"What?" said Bean.

"We've got to send it back to its grave," said Ivy. "We need to expel it."

"Expel? Like Cody?" Cody had lit two garbage cans on fire and wasn't allowed to come back to school any-more. He was expelled.

"Yeah. Like Cody," said Ivy. "That'll fix everything."

"How are you going to expel a ghost?" Leo asked.

They had forgotten he was there.

"Secret," said Ivy and Bean at the same moment.

They looked at each other and smiled.

"Aw, come on," said Leo. "I won't tell."

"Can't," said Ivy as she started to walk away.

Leo looked glum. Bean felt sorry for him. "We'll tell you afterward."

"Oh, thanks," he said.

Bean turned and raced to catch up with Ivy, who was halfway up the street.

THE POTION SOLUTION

"This is going to be great!" said Bean happily. She just loved potions.

The two girls were in Ivy's magic lab. The magic lab was one of the five little rooms that Ivy had made inside her bedroom. Chalk lines on the floor showed where one room ended and another began. There was an art studio, a living room, a doll room, a sleeping area, and the lab.

Bean's favorite was the art studio, with its little white table and the stack of bins filled with markers, glitter glue, pipe cleaners, beads, colored paper, feathers, and paint. The magic lab was Ivy's favorite. In it was a book-shelf that held a shiny black rock, four fossils, a real snake skin, lots of bottles in all shapes and sizes, and jars of herbs and ingredients. Ivy loved to say "ingredients." There was another table, which Ivy had covered in tinfoil. On top was a plastic tub of water. Ivy had wanted a

sink, but her mother
had said no way, so
Ivy filled the plastic tub
in the bathroom and car-
ried it back to her lab. It
spilled a lot.

Ivy took her magic
book from its special
hiding place and began
flipping through the pages.
"There's got to be a potion in
here somewhere," she said,
frowning. Then she giggled.
"Here's one for making someone fall in love with you."

Bean made a throwing-
up sound.

"Here's one for getting your money back
after it's stolen."

"That's not it," said Bean, sticking her hand in the water tub. Some water spilled onto the floor.

"I know," said Ivy, still flipping pages, "but I don't see—here's another one for making someone fall in love with you. That's dumb. How come there's nothing for returning a ghost to its grave?"

"There should be," said Bean. "Most people don't want ghosts hanging around the house."

Ivy looked up from her book. "I wouldn't mind."

"What if it creaked open your closet door in the middle of the night," asked Bean, "and you could hear it breathing?"

Ivy thought. "I'd talk to it. My grandma's cousin lived in a house with a ghost that whistled. My grandma said that when she was a girl, she always heard the ghost whistling upstairs when she went to play at her cousin's."

"I'd freak. Was she scared?" asked Bean.

"Grandma says the only thing she's scared of is chickens, but I think she's joking. I wish I'd been there," said Ivy. "I would have asked it why it was haunting the house."

Bean stared at her hand in the water tub. It looked ghostly. "I bet ghosts are scared of themselves. It must be weird to look down and see through yourself."

Ivy looked at her. "Maybe. Maybe Grandma's ghost whistled because it was trying to cheer itself up." She went back to looking at her book, and the magic lab was quiet for a minute or two. "Hey!" she said suddenly. "Here's something that could work.

It's a potion that you pour in front of your house to keep evil spirits away."

Bean was feeling sorry for the ghost now. "But it's not an evil spirit," she argued. "It just wants the school to get off its grave. The ghost was there first. First come, first served."

"Yeah. You're right," Ivy agreed. "But the ghost has got to go. Ms. Aruba-Tate said. And besides, we'll be doing a good deed for the ghost, in a way. Don't you think it would rather be in its grave?"

Bean thought. "I guess so. That bathroom is nasty."

"Right. So here's what we'll do," Ivy leaned over the tinfoil, "we'll make a ceremony. We'll tell it that we know it's not evil. We'll tell it that we just want it to rest peacefully. We'll tell it—"

"That we come as friends," Bean said, bouncing in her chair.

"We could chant," said Ivy. "*We come as friends*," she chanted.

"*We come in peace*," chanted Bean. "A dance might be good, too," she added.

"Once it goes back to its grave, we'll pour the potion around the edges of the bathroom so it can't come back," Ivy said.

"Sounds good," said Bean. She thought for a minute. "Hey, I have an idea. You know the Egyptians?"

Ivy nodded. "Yeah?"

"They used to put presents in the grave with the dead person. Stuff to play with. And money. We should do that." Presents would make the ceremony even better.

"Presents," Ivy repeated. "That's a great idea. It'll be like an ancient burial." Suddenly, she stood up. "But first we need to make the potion."

SNEAKY BEAN

"BEAN!"

"She sounds like one of those screaming monkeys," said Ivy, stirring.

"She looks like one, too," said Bean. "Do we need more rosemary?"

"Sure," Ivy said. "Put some more in."

"BEAN! YOU'VE GOT TO COME HOME NOW! MOM SAYS."

"She's too lazy to walk across the street," said Bean. "My mom tells her to go get me, and she just stands on the porch and screams."

"She's lazy," Ivy agreed. She looked at the jars on her shelf. She had a little bit of nutmeg, and a lot of seeds she had found in the backyard. She had some dead bugs. She had plenty of baking soda. The problem with making potions from her magic book was that she never had exactly the right ingredients. Sometimes she didn't even know what they were. The keeping-away-evil-spirits potion had an ingredient called "ponie." Ivy didn't think they meant a real pony. She didn't have a pony, anyway. "I think we should put in some more baking soda," she said.

"BEAN! YOU HAD BETTER NOT MAKE ME COME GET YOU!"

Bean opened Ivy's window and leaned out. Nancy was standing on the porch,

her face red from screaming. "I'll be there in a minute!" Bean said in her regular voice.

"WHAT?" screeched Nancy.

"I'll be there in a minute," Bean called a little louder.

"There's one more thing we need," said Ivy, looking at the book again. She giggled.

"I CAN'T HEAR YOU, BUT YOU'D BETTER GET OVER HERE RIGHT NOW OR YOU'LL BE SORRY."

"I'M ALREADY SORRY ABOUT HOW STUPID YOU LOOK IN THOSE SHORTS!" Bean bellowed.

There was a tiny silence, and then Bean's front door banged shut. Nancy was going to tell their mom.

"Sheesh," said Bean. "She's so touchy. But I guess I should go home. My mom will be mad if she has to come get me."

"Okay," said Ivy. "I can do the rest by myself. But you have to get the last ingredient." She giggled again. "It's the most important one."

"What is it?" said Bean, looking around for her shoes.

"The hair of an enemy," said Ivy.

A big grin spread over Bean's face. "How much?"

"Not much." Ivy said. "Just a handful."

They looked at each other and began to laugh.

When Bean woke up, it was dark. She sat up and peered out the window. Wow, she thought. I did it. Outside, a streetlight shone down on a car and the empty sidewalk. Everyone was asleep. Even though she hadn't really expected to wake up in the middle of the night, Bean had placed a pair of scissors on the table beside her bed. She took hold of them, pointy end down, and began the tiptoe walk down the hall to Nancy's room.

It was funny to be awake when her parents weren't. There were shadows wavering on the walls. Bean began to feel a little scared. It wasn't that she was scared she'd get caught. It was more scary not to be caught. How could her parents not know that she was up?

Nancy liked her door closed at night. Bean had always thought that was weird. But now it was just plain annoying, because Bean had to open the door without making a sound. Very, very slowly, she turned the knob.

Quietly, quietly, she pushed the door. It gave one sharp creak and then swung open.

Nancy kept her door closed, but she kept her curtain open. This was very handy, because the streetlight coming in the open window gave Bean enough light to see. Nancy was rolled into a ball under her blanket, and her long brown hair was spilled out over her pillow. Every once in a while, she gave a long, sniffy breath. Bean almost laughed. This was going to be easy-peasy.

But it wasn't as easy as she thought. Bean stood over Nancy's bed for a long time. She could have cut almost all of Nancy's hair off. It was lying right there. But Bean knew she wasn't going to do that. That would be meaner than anything she had ever done. And besides, she'd get caught. No, what Bean had to decide was whether she wanted Nancy to know her hair had been cut. If Bean took one piece and cut it way up near Nancy's head, it could be a couple of weeks before she noticed it, but then it would bug her for a long time. On the other hand, if Bean just trimmed

off a little all the way across the bottom, Nancy probably wouldn't notice at all.

Bean sighed softly. She should just trim it. This was

what Ms. Aruba-Tate called making a mature decision. Mature decisions were not as much fun as immature decisions, but sometimes you had to make them.

Bean leaned over the pillow and began to snip very, very quietly.

NO SUCH THING

Food coloring didn't change the magic of a potion. It just made it look better. Most potions, Ivy had learned, came out greenish brown. Sometimes, they were pinkish brown, which was even worse. So Ivy fixed them up with food coloring.

"Wow," said Bean, when she saw the thick blue liquid in Ivy's jar. "That's really blue. How much did you put in?"

"Almost a whole thingie."

"Doesn't your mom get mad when you do that?" asked Bean. But she knew the answer. Ivy's mom didn't get mad about using things up. She got mad about messes. All parents were different.

"Did you get the hair?" Ivy asked.

"Yeah." Bean pulled a plastic bag out of her pocket. "It's just little bits. She didn't even notice." Even though that's what Bean had wanted, she had still been disappointed.

Ivy understood. "Maybe she'll notice later."

The two girls crouched down and carefully

added the bits of hair to the jar. After they put the lid back on, they took turns shaking the jar until the hair was mixed in. Then Ivy whispered some magic words while Bean plugged her ears. Even with the oath of liquids, Bean wasn't supposed to hear Ivy's magic words.

When she was done, Ivy put the jar in her backpack. The girls started walking to school. "Did you bring a present for the ghost?" Ivy asked.

"I'm going to give it my half-dollar," said Bean, showing a bright silver coin. "What about you?"

"I brought one of my fossils. The shell one."

"That's a good present for a ghost." Fossils and ghosts were both leftovers of dead things.

When the girls got to Emerson School, Leo was waiting for them. "Are you guys still going to expel the ghost?" he asked.

"Of course. We made a potion," said Bean.

Leo shook his head. "You guys are nuts," he said. But then he asked, "What's in it?"

"Secret," said Bean.

"All we can tell you is that this potion is very powerful," said Ivy in a mysterious voice. "And at lunch recess, the ghost will be expelled. Never to return."

Leo dropped his ball and gave it a soft kick. "I'll help if you want."

By morning recess, all the kids in the second grade knew that Ivy and Bean were going to expel the ghost at lunch. Everyone gathered around the play structure again.

"Ms. Aruba-Tate said you weren't supposed to talk about the ghost anymore, Ivy," said Zuzu. She snapped the waist of her skirt.

"That's not what she said," Ivy said. "She said she expected that she wouldn't hear any more nonsense about a ghost in the bathroom."

"And she's not going to because we're going to expel it with our potion," added Bean.

"That's why we're doing it," said Ivy. "For Ms. Aruba-Tate. If it was just us, we wouldn't. We don't mind it."

"My uncle knows a guy who saw a ghost, and his hair turned white in one second!" said Eric.

"Ghosts are dead!" said Drew. "They're going to eat your brains!"

Ivy and Bean rolled their eyes. "That's zombies," said Bean.

"The ghost was here first," Ivy said, trying to be patient. "The school invaded its resting place. We have to send it back to its grave, but we're going to give it presents like the Egyptians did with their dead people. It's going to be a ceremony."

Zuzu snapped her waistband again and said, "Well, I don't believe in ghosts, and I'm going to tell Ms. Aruba-Tate what you're doing." She turned toward the classroom.

Uh-oh, thought Bean. Trouble.

"HALT!" It was Ivy's voice, louder than anyone (but Bean) had ever heard it.

Zuzu halted.

Ivy glared at Zuzu. "You have insulted the ghost of Emerson School. The ghost is now your enemy!"

Zuzu's face got bright pink. "No it's not! There's no such thing as ghosts!"

Quickly, before Ivy could get really mad, Bean said, "Don't worry, Zuzu. We're going to expel the ghost. We've got a potion."

"I'm not worried," Zuzu said in a high voice, "but she said it was my enemy, and she's not supposed to talk about it."

"It's not your enemy, I promise," said Bean firmly. "She was just kidding." She looked hard at Ivy.

Ivy smiled sweetly. "But if you wanted to make extra sure, you could give it a present, too. Just to be on the safe side."

"What?" said Zuzu.

"You could give the ghost a present," said Ivy. "For it to carry to the grave. Just in case there is such a thing as ghosts."

Zuzu stared at Ivy. "I don't have a present."

Ivy looked her over. "That hairclip is nice," she said.

Zuzu thought for a moment, and then she unhooked her pink butterfly hairclip. "You can have it. I have lots of better ones at home," she said, giving it to Ivy.

"I'm sure the ghost will like it a lot. Even if it doesn't have any hair," said Bean.

"It can use it for decoration," said Ivy.

The bell rang.

IN THE HAUNTED BATHROOM

The second grade ate its lunch faster than ever before. Dusit choked on his sandwich and almost threw up, but then Eric hit him on the back. After that, he was fine.

Ivy couldn't eat her lunch at all. Bean only ate her cookies.

Soon, all of the second grade and some of the first grade gathered around the play structure. They stared at Ivy and Bean and the jar of blue potion in Ivy's hand.

The two girls started toward the haunted bathroom. About twenty kids followed along to watch. When they got to the breezeway where the bathroom was, everyone sat down on the benches along the sides.

Bean started to feel a little sweaty. She tried to think about Ms. Aruba-Tate saying that the bathroom wasn't haunted. But she kept thinking about an army of ghosts.

There was the portal.

There was the bathroom door.

It was just her and Ivy. And Leo.

"Leo's going in the girls' bathroom!" hollered Eric from the bench.

"Leo's a girl!" yelled Dusit.

Leo gave a little jump and said, "I'm not going in, you goons. I'm keeping watch." Turning to Ivy and Bean, he said, "If the Yard Duty comes, I'll throw the ball at the door."

They nodded.

Ivy took a deep breath, reached out, and pushed the door open.

Together, Ivy and Bean entered the bathroom.

+ + + + + +

Inside was dim and quiet. Bean noticed that it smelled better than it usually did.

"Do you feel it?" said Ivy, looking around.

Nothing happened. After a moment, Bean stopped feeling sweaty. She was glad there wasn't an army, but she wanted to see one ghost at least. She squinted and then popped her eyes out. There. "Yes," she said. "And I see the mist." A thin cloud was just fading in the corner. They stood still. "Do you hear something?" Bean whispered.

It was a smooth, sighing sound. It sounded as if it was coming from very far away. "I hear it," Ivy whispered.

That was a little spooky. Bean began to feel sweaty again.

"We'd better start chanting," Ivy breathed. Noise would help.

"Yeah," said Bean. "We come in peace," she whispered.

"We come in peace!" said Ivy loudly. She raised her hands to the ceiling and fluttered her fingers down.

Bean fluttered her fingers, too. "Oh, ghost friend! Haunt our school no more!" Her voice was louder now.

"Lie peacefully under our school!" wailed Ivy. That was better. The bathroom wasn't spooky anymore. She began to turn in circles, waving her hands.

Now Bean whirled around, too, shouting, "Take our respectful greeting and fly away!" This was getting fun.

"Farewell!" shrieked Ivy, spinning faster and faster. "Return to your resting place, and we will honor you forever!" She jumped a few times. "Begone!"

"Leave the bathroom of Emerson School!" screamed Bean. She did a few high kicks.

"Leave the bathroom of Emerson School!" screamed Ivy, jumping and whirling. She banged into one of the stall doors. "Ow!"

Bean was still spinning. The bathroom zoomed around her. Whew. She stopped and held onto a stall. "Can we do the potion now?" she asked.

Ivy unscrewed the lid of the jar and crouched down. The bathroom grew quiet. "Ghost, begone," she murmured and poured a line of potion in front of the door. She crawled around the edges of the bathroom, pouring.

"Begone," Bean chanted softly.

Ivy stuck her hand in something wet. "Oh, yuck," she said.

The bathroom was very quiet now. Peaceful. Three stalls down, one to go. It took

a lot of concentration to pour evenly. Ivy made sure that she got every corner. The bright blue potion gleamed on the tile, and Ivy stopped under the paper towel dispenser to look at her work. It was pretty. She looked up. No mist. No sighing noise. The bathroom looked normal, except for the blue potion. The ghost was gone. "I think we did it," she said, peering around.

Bean squinted. "Is it gone?"

"Yes," said Ivy. "Expelled. Never to return."

"I'm sort of sad that it's over," said Bean. "It was fun having a haunted bathroom."

"But we still have to do the presents," said
Ivy, taking her fossil and Zuzu's hairclip out
of her pocket.

Bean took out her half-dollar. "How are
we going to—" she began.

And then there was a bang on the door.

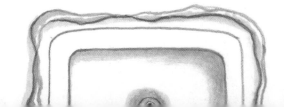

EXPELLED

It was Leo's soccer ball.

Bean started for the door.

"No! No! The presents!" hissed Ivy. She stuffed the jar in the trash can and rushed into a stall.

Bean rushed after her. "What're you doing?!"

Ivy was throwing the fossil and Zuzu's hairclip into the toilet. "Give me your half-dollar," she said. "Quick!"

Bean handed it to her. Ivy threw that into the toilet, too. "But why are you putting them in the—?" Bean began.

The bathroom door wheezed open.

"How else are we going to get them underground?" Ivy whispered. She flushed.

"Come out here this instant!"

They knew that voice. It wasn't Rose the Yard Duty. It was Mrs. Noble.

Ivy and Bean came out of the stall. Mrs. Noble's wrinkles were all pointing downward in a terrible frown. "Just what do you think you're doing in here?!" she boomed.

"Going to the bathroom?" said Ivy. It was all she could think of. She glanced at Bean. Help!

"There are thirty children huddled out in the hall staring at this bathroom like it's a television. I know you're up to something!" Mrs. Noble snapped. "You can tell me, or you can tell the Principal!" She reached out and grabbed Bean by the shoulder. Her fingers were like claws.

"We just had to—to—" Bean had no idea what she was going to say next.

Then they heard something.

A groan.

A grinding. A gurgling.

A sound of water.

And then, from the toilet, a river of water came spilling and splashing over the side and onto the tiles. There was a lot of it, and it didn't stop coming. Something under the floor was making a lot of noise.

The water ran over the sides of the toilet and streamed across the tile floor. Mrs. Noble let go of Bean's shoulder and took a step backward. The water flowed toward her red high heels, and she stepped back again.

"We heard the toilet making a funny noise," said Ivy, watching the water roll across the floor. "We were trying to fix it when you came in."

"But it's still broken," said Bean.

The toilet water sloshed around their shoes.

"It's kind of gross, isn't it?" said Ivy to Mrs. Noble.

"At least there's no you-know-what in it," said Bean.

Mrs. Noble didn't answer. She hopped backward, but the water touched her

red high heels anyway. "Disgusting!" She hopped. "Disgusting! I'll call the janitor! Uck!" She hopped again, yanked the door open, and was gone.

Ivy and Bean stepped into the breezeway, their shoes making wet marks on the cement. Leo was leaning against the wall with his soccer ball under his arm.

Most of the others were still sitting on the benches.

"Well?" said Emma. "What happened?"

"The ghost has been expelled," said Ivy. "But it wasn't easy."

"Mrs. Noble *ran*," said Vanessa.

Bean shrugged. "She was scared. She couldn't take it."

"Well, she came in during a very scary part," Ivy said. "That ghost really wanted to stay in the bathroom."

"What did it look like?" Eric asked.

Ivy looked at Bean. "Strange. Pale."

Bean looked at Ivy. "Almost like water."

"Like water?" said Emma. "Weird."

"So it's gone?" said Zuzu. "For good?"

"Yes," said Ivy. "But I wouldn't go in there for a while."

"The bathroom got kind of messed up," said Bean.

The second-graders looked toward the bathroom door. They were quiet, thinking about the bathroom and Mrs. Noble and the ghost.

"Come on," said Eric. "There's a little more recess left."

They started walking down the breeze-way. Ivy and Bean sat down on a bench.

Leo looked at them. "So what really happened in there?" he asked.

"Secret," said Bean.

Leo bounced the soccer ball hard against the cement and caught it. "Hey. I was the one who warned you that Mrs. Noble was coming."

Bean looked at Ivy. Ivy looked out at the playground, where the second-graders were getting back to their regular lunch-recess stuff. Eric was chasing Drew. Mikayla and Vanessa were pulling on a jump rope. The kindergartners were grinding rocks. Emma and Zuzu were practicing cartwheels again. Only Leo had stayed. "Okay. We'll tell you."

Leo slitted his eyes. "Was there a ghost in there, really?"

"Yes," said Ivy.

"Totally," said Bean.

Leo glanced from one to the other. "And that's why Mrs. Noble ran?"

Ivy looked at the sky. "Well, actually, Mrs. Noble ran because the toilet overflowed on her shoes."

"The toilet overflowed on her shoes?" Leo said. "How come?"

"Ivy flushed the ghost's presents down the toilet," explained Bean.

"You flushed a fossil?" Leo laughed.

"And a half-dollar and a hairclip. It seemed like the best way to send them,"

Ivy said. "We didn't have time to dig a hole."
She giggled. It was kind of funny.

"You guys are wacko!" said Leo, laughing.

The three of them walked down to the playground together.

"Hey, Leo, how do you play soccer, anyway?" asked Bean. "I'm getting kind of sick of gymnastics."

"I never really liked gymnastics very much," said Ivy. "I can't do cartwheels."

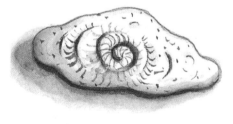

WHAT A GREAT DAY

What a great day, Bean thought. She was eating her ice cream on the front porch. She stirred hard, watching the chocolate part swirl into the vanilla part. Yum. Ice-cream soup.

Ivy stepped out onto her front porch, holding an ice-cream bar.

"Come over!" yelled Bean.

Ivy went back inside and came out after a moment. She started down the steps, stopping every few feet to lick the drips from her bar.

"What do you have?" she asked as she sat down next to Bean.

"Ice-cream soup," said Bean, showing her. "Mm."

They ate in silence for a few minutes. Then—*bang*—the porch door slammed shut behind Nancy.

"You spilled on your shirt," she said to Bean.

Bean looked down. She had spilled on her shirt. "Oh well," she said.

Nancy sat down. "It'll never come out," she said. "Mom says you have to come in and do your math."

"Hi, Nancy," said Ivy.

"Hi," said Nancy in a not-very-friendly way. "You're supposed to go in, Bean."

"Okay," said Bean without getting up.

"Did you get a new haircut, Nancy?" Ivy asked.

"What? No," said Nancy. There was a pause. "Why? Does my hair look different?"

Bean stared very hard at her milkshake.

Ivy licked a drip. "Yeah." She tilted her head to the side and looked at Nancy's hair. "The bottom—there— it looks different. Kind of uneven. You know?"

"It does?" said Nancy, grabbing some hair and pulling it in front of her face.

"Yeah. Sort of uneven," Ivy said. She cracked off a piece of chocolate coating and ate it.

Nancy stared at her hair and then got up and went inside.

Ivy and Bean finished their ice cream in silence.

A really great day, thought Bean.

SNEAK PREVIEW OF BOOK 3
IVY + BEAN
BREAK THE FOSSIL RECORD

Boring.

Boring!

Boring!

Bean turned her book upside down and tried to read it that way. Cool. Well, sort of cool. No. Boring.

Bean sighed and turned her book back right side up. It was a book about cats she had picked from the school library. There was a different cat on each page. Bean liked cats, but reading about them was driving her crazy. All the cats looked the same except the sphynx cat, who didn't have any fur. He looked halfway between a dog and a rat. Bean liked him the best.

I bet Ivy's never seen a sphynx cat, thought Bean. She knew she wasn't supposed to talk during Drop Everything and Read, so she poked Ivy in the ribs.

But Ivy's eyes were binging across the pages of her book. Bing, bing, bing. She looked like she was watching a Ping-Pong game. She didn't even notice Bean.

So Bean poked her again. "Hey!" she whispered. "Earth to Ivy!"

"Hmm?" Ivy mumbled.

"Looky here! It's a dog-rat!" Bean whispered louder.

Ivy looked for a little tiny second. "Oh," she said, and went back to reading.

Bean sighed again. All the other children in Ms. Aruba-Tate's second-grade classroom were bent over their books. Even Eric, who usually fell out of his chair two or three times during

Drop Everything and Read, was quiet. He had a book about man-eating sharks.

MacAdam was picking his nose. Bean raised her hand. Ms. Aruba-Tate didn't see because she was reading, too, so Bean called out, "Ms. Aruba-Tate!"

"Shhh," whispered Ms. Aruba-Tate. "What is it, Bean?"

"There's a problem and it starts with *M*," began Bean, looking hard at MacAdam. "And then *N* and *P*." She wiggled her finger next to her nose, just in case Ms. Aruba-Tate needed an extra hint.

Ms. Aruba-Tate looked at MacAdam, too. Then she put down her book and came over to Bean's table. "I brought this from home especially for you, Bean," she said, holding out a big, shiny book. "See," she pointed at the cover. "It's *The Amazing Book of World*

Records. I think you'll like it."

Bean wasn't sure. "What's a world record?"

"When someone does something better or longer or weirder than anyone else in the whole world, that means they've set a world record."

"Weirder?" Bean asked. That sounded interesting.

Ms. Aruba-Tate smiled. "There's a man in here who walked on his hands for eight hundred and seventy miles."

"You mean on his hands and knees? Like a baby?"

"No, just on his hands. With his feet in the air," said Ms. Aruba-Tate.

"No way."

"Read the book. You'll see." Ms. Aruba-Tate returned to her chair.

Bean opened the shiny cover. On the very first page there was a picture of a woman whose black hair trailed behind her like a fancy cape. Bean read that the hair was 19 feet long, and that the woman had been growing it since she was 12. Wow, thought Bean. Doesn't it get dirt and bugs in it? Bean turned the page. Eeeew. A man was eating a scorpion. Double-eeeew! He ate 30 scorpions a day! On the next page was a picture of a boy with 256 straws in his mouth! What did his mouth look like when there were no straws in it? Big and slobbery, Bean guessed.

"Ivy!" she whispered. "Ivy!"

Ivy's eyes stopped binging back and forth. "What?"

"Check this out!"

"He stuck one hundred and fifty-nine clothes-pins on his face!" shouted Eric. "Look at him!"

It was recess, but instead of soccer or jump rope or monkey bars, the second-graders were huddled under the play structure. At the center of the circle were Bean and her book. Kids pulled the book back and forth, all trying to look at the pages at the same time.

"Look at her! Ninety-nine hula hoops at once!" Vanessa squeaked. "Around her neck, too!"

"Look at this turnip! It weighs thirty-nine pounds!" said Dusit.

"Gross! I hate turnips," Eric said. "My mom made me eat one once, and I spit it into the heater."

"I hate lima beans," said Dusit.

Bean pulled the book back in her direction. After all, Ms. Aruba-Tate had brought it especially for her. "This guy broke more bones than any living human," read Bean. In the picture, he was smiling happily. "He's broken his leg fourteen times."

"On purpose?" asked Emma.

"I guess so," said Bean. "He jumps off of buildings."

Drew slid the book his way. "Hey! This guy collects teeth! He has two million teeth!"

"This is the world's most poisonous snake," read Leo, pointing to another picture. "It's called the carpet viper."

"Does it live in carpets?" asked Zuzu. She looked worried.

"In India and Africa," said Leo. "Not here."

Bean slid the book back her way. "Look, Zuzu! This girl did one hundred and nine cartwheels in a row."

"Let me see that!" Zuzu grabbed the book and looked closely at the picture of a teenage girl in tights. "I bet I could do one hundred and ten."

"Bet you couldn't," said Eric.